Witchin Warlock

Charity Parkerson

Punk & Sissy Publications

—Warning: This book is intended for readers over the age of 18.

Editor: BZ Hercules & Consultants

Cover designer: 100 Covers

Contents

Introduction

CASPIAN COMES FROM A long line of witches. Brock is third generation F.B.I. They shouldn't fit, but they do.

A year ago, Caspian moved to a small town in Ohio. He hoped the lack of competition in the area would be good for his psychic business, Futures Untold. The last thing he expected was a sexy F.B.I. agent to show up and treat him like a missing person's bloodhound. Even though Caspian keeps doing favors for Special Agent Brock Wray, his distrust of authority runs deep. After all, they used to drown witches in this area back in the day, and Caspian has no desire to end up on Brock's missing persons' list.

Officially, no one knows how Brock keeps solving so many huge cases. Caspian is Brock's secret weapon. The man knows things no one should. That's not why Brock keeps showing up and making excuses to see Caspian. Caspian fascinates Brock. Not only does Brock's inner detective need to know how Caspian knows so much, but Caspian is also smoking hot. He is the single most gorgeous man to step foot in their tiny town in ages. Brock isn't dumb. He has to take Caspian off the market as quickly as possible and he'll use any excuse to get close enough to do it.

When Brock takes Caspian along for the ride on a case, things will get weird. Let's hope Caspian isn't forced to show why he's the most witchin warlock around or Brock might run for the hills.

Witchin Warlock is a fun short story just in time for Halloween.

EVERY GOOD WITCH, WIZARD, warlock, psychic, medium, or whatever a person chose to identify as knew New Orleans was the place to be to showcase the best powers. However, there were a few issues with that way of thinking. For one, New Orleans was hot. It smelled funny, and every witch, wizard, warlock, psychic, and medium knew it was the place to be to freely showcase their magic. That meant competition out the wazoo. So, when Caspian's great aunt—the one and only Magical Margo—died and left Caspian her Tarot and Medium shoppe, Caspian immediately sold out and headed north.

Even real spell casters needed a shtick if they hoped to drum up clientele. Margo had talked to ghosts. People had come from far and wide to talk to their children, parents, and spouses on the other side. Margo hadn't been a real medium. She had been a real witch, and she had taught Caspian that with the right spell, anything was possible. Unfortunately, Caspian didn't have what it took to comfort grieving family members. What Caspian could do was predict the future with flair, and—

unfortunately—he could also catch the eye of the Ohio branch office of the F.B.I.

That was why Special Agent Brock Wray currently stared a hole in the side of Caspian's head while Caspian finished with his client, Clara. Clara came to him each week. All she really wanted was a friend to chat with. Despite that, she had paid to be there. Brock had not, so Brock could just wait with his fancy hair and too tight suit. Goddamn. It was getting kind of hot inside his shop.

"I know you said my soulmate has dark brown hair, but Chad has blond hair, and I really think he's the one."

“No one named Chad is ever the one,” Caspian said, barely hanging on to his temper, with Brock still staring at him.

Brock chuckled and then tried covering the sound with a cough.

Caspian had been in Elvenwood, Ohio for almost a year and had a good clientele. He loved Clara dearly. She paid him good money for these weekly chats, but she was also dumb as a box of rocks. He could tell her the first and last name of her soulmate. Hell, with the right spell work, Caspian could give her the guy’s social security number. What he couldn’t do was make her quit falling for every loser along the way.

Clara's brown eyes narrowed. She rubbed her chin. "You know, I have thought it was a little weird that Chad doesn't answer his phone past a certain time each night. He says his wife left him last year, and he has his small kids, so he doesn't want the phone waking them, but it's weird. Like all he has to do is turn off his ringer and check it occasionally. It's not fucking rocket science. There's no need to disappear from the planet all because the kids are asleep."

Brock sat forward, as if really getting into the conversation. "You're not talking about Chad Bowman, are you?"

Clara twisted in her seat. "Yeah. Do you know him?"

Brock nodded. “I picked him up on Grindr six months ago. His wife didn’t leave him. She’s pregnant with his fourth kid. He tried to pull that same shit on me, but I investigate everyone I date.”

“Are you fucking kidding me? That rat bastard.”

That was the thing about a small town. It was hard to get away with anything. Too many people knew each other.

Clara looked Caspian’s way. Her shoulders fell. “I guess you’re right. It’s not him.”

Caspian nodded. “Dark hair. Look out for dark hair. He also has blue eyes, if that helps. I sense you've already met, but you've been too preoccupied to notice. Make sure you open your mind. You'll find him. He's already noticed you."

Clara brightened. "Really? Well, I guess I'd better go. I have to dump Chad before my shift starts at the store. Next week, same time?"

"I've got you on my calendar," Caspian assured her as he stood and walked her to the door. They hugged and said their final goodbyes before Caspian turned his attention Brock's way. "So you picked up Chad on Grindr? Special Agent Wray, I never would have guessed."

Brock's dark blue eyes flashed with humor. "In my defense, who hasn't thought someone named Chad was the one?"

"Fair," Caspian said, clearing away his tarot cards. They were useless to him. He only used them for show. Every snippet Caspian saw of the future came from a potion he drank before each appointment. "What brings you my way, agent?"

Brock's mouth lifted in one corner in a sexy smirk. Caspian hated that he noticed. His entire life, Margo had drilled into his head a mistrust of authorities. He had a gift. Normal people would use him for it. People like Brock would have him committed. After all, it was the authorities that used to drown witches in these parts.

"You don't like me, do you?" Brock said, as if reading Caspian's mind.

Caspian pasted on a bright smile, refusing to admit any such thing. "What an odd thing to say. You didn't answer my question."

Brock shook his head and sighed. "We have a missing person. A local bus driver didn't show up for his route. Sheriff Kennedy went to his house. The door was open, but there didn't seem to be anything missing. There was no sign of the guy. His bus and personal vehicle were still in the driveway. His wallet was on the dresser and his shoes were by the door. It's like he simply vanished. After a search of the local area, Lonnie called me."

A smile snapped to Caspian's lips without his permission. "It must be a slow day at the F.B.I. if I was the first person you thought to visit."

Brock held his stare. Caspian's skin tingled with awareness of the other man's large presence in his tiny shop. "I'm not here on behalf of the bureau. I'm just a concerned citizen today, looking for a neighbor."

Caspian's eyebrows rose. "And you came to me? I don't know any bus drivers."

"You know things, Caspian. Don't pretend you don't. You've helped out law enforcement in the past. No one knows the things you do. Hell, I'm willing to bet money you know the name of Clara's soulmate, but you're not saying so you can milk her for every dime."

"A man has to eat," Caspian shot back, unashamed.

A slow smile spread across Brock's lips, making it a little harder for Caspian to breathe. He really fucking hated that he found Brock so hot. "Who is it?"

"Scott." Damn it. He could kick himself. It was like Brock had some magical hold on Caspian's dumb brain.

A bark of laughter burst from Brock. "The manager at the grocery store?"

Caspian nodded. "He's her boss, so he doesn't want to make a move, and she's too busy with the Chads of the world to notice he's sickeningly in love with her."

Brock's bright smile slipped away. "Help me, Caspian. I won't tell anyone how you do it."

A sigh gathered in Caspian's throat. Caspian swallowed it down. He was such a sucker for blue eyes and nice shoulders. "Fine. I need something of his." His spell was wearing off from his visit with Clara. He hadn't expected to do two readings today without a recharge.

Brock visibly tried hiding his triumph as he passed a set of keys with a fake rabbit's foot attached Caspian's way.

Caspian's fingers wrapped around the keys. He took a breath and closed his eyes. Immediately, the vision of a yellow school bus speeding past waiting children filled Caspian's head. Then it was gone. He didn't get more. The effects of his earlier potion were gone. Still, that was odd.

Caspian tilted his head to one side and considered what he had seen. "I thought you said his bus was still in the driveway."

"It is. Why?"

"Huh." Caspian shook his head. "I need more time. My visions aren't making sense. I'll need to commune with the dead." He wanted Brock to think he was strange. Caspian didn't know why. He just enjoyed seeing how much bullshit Brock would swallow to get his next lead.

To Caspian's surprise, Brock smiled. "Fine. Keep the keys. I'll pick you up around... seven?"

Caspian blinked. "For what?"

"Our date," Brock said, as if they had discussed the matter a dozen times. "The fall festival starts at five, but I'd rather let things die down a bit. I don't want to fight a crowd of kids."

"Um..."

"See you at seven," Brock said as he headed for the door.

Caspian stared at the front door of his shop for five minutes after Brock left. His mind grappled with the idea of dating an F.B.I. agent. No good could come of that. That ass, though. Brock's did look firm. What the fuck was he supposed to do now?

A smile pulled at the corners of Brock's mouth, making his cheeks ache as he left Caspian's shop, Futures Untold. He loved the disgruntled way Caspian always tolerated his presence. It always put a little extra pep in his step, keeping Caspian off guard. All the gay men for three towns around had their sights set on the brown-eyed beauty. Caspian had the body of a Greek god and a smile so wicked, he nearly made Brock pant the first time they met. Brock couldn't explain why he enjoyed Caspian's irritation so much, but he always felt closer to winning him when Caspian growled at him. He knew he shouldn't claim they had a date until he actually had Caspian outside his shop, but they had a date. He couldn't wait. Elvenwood's annual Halloween Fall Festival was the best around, and this was Brock's favorite season. He loved everything about Halloween. The air had a certain scent. He wasn't a fan of kids, but he remembered the excitement of dressing up and getting candy from strangers. Brock loved staying up, eating junk, and watching scary movies. There was an excitement in the air. He should probably feel a little guilty for using Frank Steeler's disappearance as a reason to see Caspian, but that was part and parcel with his profession. Everything was doom and gloom. At least, this way, some good came from the everyday wretchedness. He was dying to know what happened to Frank, though. The guy had lived in this town his whole life. He had been a bus driver for forty years without missing a day. It made no sense for him to vanish without a trace.

"Hey there, Agent Wray. Can we expect to see you tonight at the festival?"

Brock slid into his usual booth at Clark's diner. "I'll be there."

His waitress, Debbie, had been asking him the same question every day at lunch for a week. His answer never changed. He knew she hoped for more, but he never gave in. Brock very decidedly swung the other way.

"Would you like your regular?"

He flashed the buxom blonde a smile. "Please and thank you." He knew he was a little boring and could probably save money by packing the same thing for lunch every day rather than ordering it, but he liked the atmosphere at Clark's. Not to mention, Brock lived alone and spent a good eighty percent of his time by himself. It was nice to have some interaction with other people.

Debbie brought him his usual tea and veggie sandwich. "I heard Mr. Steeler has gone missing. Do you have any leads?"

Even though Brock technically shouldn't talk about any cases outside the office, in this case, there was nothing to tell. "Not yet."

"I'm surprised you didn't learn anything from Caspian. That boy, if I didn't know better, I'd swear he really is psychic."

First off, this town never ceased to amaze him. He had just left Caspian's shop, and everyone already knew where he had been. Second, it was hilarious to him to hear Debbie call Caspian a boy when they were likely the same age. Last, she wasn't wrong. More than once, Brock had mused over Caspian's abilities. They were uncanny. But at the end of the day, Brock didn't really believe in all that nonsense.

"He's definitely highly intuitive. In this case, though, I think it'll take him some time to wade through the intricacies of the case."

Debbie nodded. Her ponytail bobbed along with her head. She didn't leave him alone to eat. His discomfort grew. “Speaking of tonight’s festival…”

Fuck.

“I was thinking…”

Goddamn it.

The bell above the door jingled as it was shoved open harder than necessary. All heads turned that way. An aggravated-looking Caspian glanced over his shoulder at the bell like it was to blame for his over-the-top entrance. Brock hid a smile. He found everything about Caspian adorable.

Caspian scanned the diner. His gaze landed on Brock, and he barreled

Brock's way. Debbie took a step back as Caspian plopped down across from Brock and slapped Frank's keys down on the table. "He's dead."

Debbie gasped.

Caspian tossed her a quick glance. "Oh. Hey, Deb. Could I get a Coke?"

"Of course." She raced away, obviously way more excited to tell her bit of gossip than she was about grabbing Caspian a drink.

Brock didn't bother retrieving the keys. "That didn't take long."

Caspian shrugged and stole a chip from Brock's plate. "When you handed me the keys earlier, I saw a yellow bus speeding past groups of kids waiting at their stops. That struck me as odd since you said he didn't show up for work and his bus was in the driveway. When you left, I drank some tonic."

"Tonic?"

Caspian shook his head. "Coffee."

"You said tonic."

"Well, I meant coffee," Caspian said, sounding irritated over Brock's interruptions. "Anyhow, I drank some coffee, and everything cleared in my head. When he got on the bus this morning, there was someone waiting inside, and they ambushed him. After they... did the deed, they drove him out to the old, abandoned sawmill, dumped his body, and then drove the bus back to his place."

Damn, that was... detailed. "Where were you around that time this morning?"

Caspian didn't as much as flinch, even though he had to know it was suspicious for him to know that much detail. "Jogging, as always. I ran into Susan Tolbert and spent thirty minutes listening to her bitch about her cheating husband. I'm sure she'd be glad to vouch for as much."

Brock's shoulders relaxed. "Yeah. Geoff's been cheating with Naomi down at the store for a few months now. To be fair, though, Susan has been sleeping with Naomi down at the store for months now too. I'm glad you have an alibi and I hope you understand why I had to ask."

Caspian shrugged and stole another chip. "I know too much. I get it. It's been like this my whole life." He popped the chip in his mouth and chewed while staring off into the distance. When he met Brock's stare again, Brock fought a sigh. He was truly beautiful, even though he looked sad. "For the record, if you plan to accuse me of something every time you ask for my help, I'd rather you not ask again. In small town terms, I haven't lived here all that long. If people start to think there's something wrong with me, my business will suffer. I don't want to have to move."

Guilt hit harder than Brock expected. In his line of work, he saw all the bad in people. This one time, he didn't want to be that guy. It wasn't fair for him to ask for Caspian's help and then crucify him for it. Brock definitely didn't want Caspian's business to suffer or for Caspian to move. He pushed his plate to the center of the table so Caspian could share. "Sorry about that. I always appreciate your help and I wouldn't come to you if I thought there was anything wrong with you. In fact, I like you a lot."

Debbie appeared with Caspian's Coke. "Can I get you anything else?"

Caspian didn't look away from Brock. "No, thank you."

Debbie left them alone, and they continued staring at each other.

"So, you really have visions, huh?"

Caspian nodded. "Yep."

"Who's your soulmate, then?"

Caspian didn't smile as Brock hoped. He shrugged. "I never look at my future."

"You should."

"Why? Do you think it's you?"

Brock nodded. "Yep."

They went back to staring at each other in silence.

Brock nudged his plate even closer. “Do you want half of my sandwich?”

“I’m a vegetarian.”

“It’s a veggie sandwich.”

“I don’t think I can eat after the things I saw.”

They dropped their gazes to Brock’s plate. Half his chips were gone. Brock didn’t call Caspian on it, and Caspian didn’t look guilty. They went back to staring at each other.

“I guess we should go find this body.”

“Better bring a shovel.”

Brock winced. “That bad, huh?”

Caspian nodded.

“Well.” Brock dug out his wallet and dropped a twenty on the table. “I still say we should get to it. The quicker we get back, the faster I can get to fucking you.”

“Okay.”

Damn. Brock had never been more excited to dig up a body in his life.

Chapter Two

THEY MADE THE DRIVE into the middle of nowhere in mostly silence. Occasionally, Caspian broke it by giving details of his vision when he recognized a landmark. Otherwise, Caspian didn't know what to say. Brock thought they were soulmates and he planned to fuck Caspian later. It had been a strange day.

When they came to the area where they would have to walk the rest of the way, they climbed from the car, donned their jackets, and Brock grabbed a shovel. They headed through the trees. It was an oddly pleasant walk, considering they were on their way to find a dead person.

Caspian couldn't stop tossing glances Brock's way. He genuinely was a gorgeous guy. Caspian had always tried avoiding those thoughts, since Brock could ruin him. Brock had seemed to believe that Caspian had powers. Caspian didn't know where to go with that. Margo had always said Caspian would know when he had met the one. He would recognize him by the man's acceptance. Now Caspian was off his game, thanks to musing over it.

Brock suddenly threw out his arm, stopping Caspian from taking another step, and pulling Caspian's mind back on track. There was an open man-sized hole in the ground. It was empty. Caspian went on high alert. Something wasn't right. Frank should be in that hole. The slightest rustling sound behind them was all the warning they got before Brock was knocked to the ground. Frank came at him, teeth gnashing. Without thinking, ancient words sprang to Caspian's lips and a blue light shot from Caspian's hands, sending Frank flying. A goddamn zombie. Caspian hadn't seen one in years. He should have known, since the moon phase was right and it was the start of the day of the dead... literally.

Brock scrambled back to his feet. "What the fuck?"

Frank leapt through the air, coming for Brock again. Caspian tackled Brock to the ground, covering his body. He ended up molded against Brock, their faces only inches apart. "Stay down. I've got this," Caspian promised. Before he could stop himself, he pressed a quick kiss to Brock's lips and rolled away. He kept his body between Brock and Frank, physically blocking Frank's advance. Frank had no interest in Caspian. Caspian didn't smell like a human. He smelled like magic, which didn't appeal to most flesh-eating beasts.

Frank shuffled closer, visibly looking for his opening to get to the only thing he cared about: food. His dead eyes and pale face didn't unnerve Caspian anywhere near as much as the massive amount of flesh missing from Frank's neck. It was obvious he had been feasted upon before being left to turn. Caspian searched for some way to protect Brock without using his magic. There was a tiny chance Brock had missed his use of magic while face down on the ground earlier. Now he had Brock's full attention. He couldn't hide.

His gaze landed on the shovel Brock had dropped when he had been attacked. Before he could lunge for the weapon, he was shoved aside. Frank sprang forward and shots rang out. The bullets slowed Frank long enough for Caspian to grab the shovel. Frank collided with Brock, taking him to the ground again. Caspian swung. The sharp edge of the shovel collided with bone and dislodged Frank's barely hanging on head. Brock shoved his way out from beneath what was left of Frank's body. His every breath came out sounding like he had just finished a marathon. He was wild-eyed and looked ready to faint.

"What the fuck?" he said between heavy breaths. "I mean, what the actual fuck?"

Caspian shook his head. “I don’t know, dude. Swamp gas?”

Brock’s crazed gaze swung Caspian’s way. “Swamp gas? Have you lost your goddamn mind? Why are you so calm? You just took off a guy’s head with a shovel. He tried to fucking eat me.”

Caspian shrugged. “He was going to hurt you. It seemed a pretty easy decision from there.”

Brock dragged his fingers through his hair, making a mess of his normally perfectly styled mane. “I have to call this in. We have to preserve the scene.” He was obviously on the verge of completely freaking out and Caspian couldn’t risk any more exposure.

Caspian dropped the shovel. He closed the space between them and claimed Brock's lips. As their tongues stroked, Caspian almost forgot to take control of Brock's mind. He hadn't expected such an amazing kiss. Damn. They were pursuing this. Later. Right now, Caspian had business.

He took a step back, leaving Brock frozen. Even though his body was on fire, he got to work. While chanting ancient spells, Caspian used the power of his blood and ancestors to move Frank's body and head back into the ground. The dirt slid into the hole, covering the body. Once the ground reclaimed the hole, grass and flowers grew, making the new grave invisible. Next, he swiped away the stains from their clothes and the shovel. Once all signs of their struggle and Frank were gone, Caspian stepped back inside Brock's hold and reclaimed his mouth.

Their tongues brushed. Brock's fingers found Caspian's hair. Caspian moaned when Brock tightened his hold on Caspian's messy locks. He almost forgot this had been a means to an end. He wanted Brock. There was no denying it.

Brock pulled away, but he didn't release Caspian. He stared at Caspian through a hooded gaze, setting Caspian's body ablaze even more than their kiss had. "Right now, we have to find that sawmill, but later..." Brock held his stare. "... later, you're mine."

Caspian's breath left his lungs. He had wanted no one more, and he hated himself for it. Brock carried a badge. No good could come of them being together. Caspian already knew he wouldn't stop, though. He wanted Brock. Nothing would stop him from having him. Something had already begun between them. There was no going back now.

Brock's body burned as they made their way through the woods toward the old, abandoned sawmill. It had been a nice day. He had no idea what had driven him to ambush Caspian with that kiss, but he regretted nothing. The sawmill came into view, and Brock went on alert. He became hyperaware he was the only protection between Caspian and a possible murderer. Brock didn't know what he had been thinking, bringing Caspian along. Caspian had told him the body had been dumped at the sawmill. He should have brought another agent with him. He had to keep Caspian safe.

Brock quietly moved a few steps ahead of Caspian and pulled out his service weapon. There were too many windows and open doorways. They could be walking into anything. Caspian seemed oddly relaxed, as if he marched into danger every day.

"There's so much rotting wood and piles of debris. You might need to come out here with dogs or ground-penetrating equipment. I doubt we'll find anything."

Caspian's claim had Brock's shoulders relaxing. It gave him the excuse he needed to get Caspian out of there before he got hurt. Caspian just knew so damn much that he seemed more capable than most. That was all the excuse Brock could muster for why he had put Caspian in danger to begin with. He would be more careful in the future. There was a bad feeling in his gut about this case. Brock had to get Caspian out of there.

"You're right. We should head back to the car."

They turned to head back the way they came. The sound of tinkling glass—like a window had shattered in the distance — sent Brock spinning back toward the building. He eyed the windows, trying to decide where the sound had come from. A quick movement by a downstairs window caught his attention. Brock focused on the spot. The outline of a head peeked out before darting out of sight again.

Brock shoved Caspian behind him. "Wait here."

Caspian didn't listen. He latched on to Brock's back and walked in step with him.

Brock cast an annoyed look over his shoulder. “I said stay put.”

“No,” Caspian whispered, as if people were listening. “If you’re putting your life in danger by not calling for backup, I’ll have to be your backup.”

Brock rolled his eyes. “How is protecting you going to help me? You’re not even armed.”

“I’m armed with charms. I’ve got you.”

Despite the seriousness of the situation, a snort escaped Brock. He liked Caspian a lot more than he had liked anyone in a long time. He definitely hadn’t dated anyone willing to put themselves in danger to guard his back. Every second they spent together; the more Brock wanted.

True to his word, Caspian stuck to Brock's back as Brock cleared the door of the sawmill. Their footsteps sounded loud in the otherwise silent building. In the years since the sawmill shut down, dust, debris, and animals had claimed the building. Sunlight streamed through the broken windows. Dust hung in the air, visible to the naked eye in the rays of light cutting through the room. Rats didn't bother hiding. Brock and Caspian were the intruders.

As they rounded the corner into the room where Brock had seen the mystery face in the window, an unnatural-sounding growl rent the air.

Birds and other small wildlife scattered. A man who looked ragged and homeless charged Brock. At the last second, Brock caught sight of the ax he held and fired. His shot hit its mark, striking the man between the eyes. For a moment, he froze. Caspian whispered something Brock couldn't hear through the ringing in his ears from the gunfire. The guy dropped. His ax flew into the air, landing perfectly to sever the man's head. Brock turned away from the sight. He sucked air, pulling years of dust into his lungs. As he fell into a coughing fit, Caspian rubbed his back.

"Now might be a good time to call this in."

He was so calm and steady. The bureau needed to hire Caspian. He had what it took.

Brock nodded. He dug his keys out and passed them Caspian's way. "Take my car and head back to town. I'll catch a ride back when all this is cleared up. You shouldn't be stuck out here the rest of the day."

Caspian cast a look around, as if assessing if it was safe to leave Brock before nodding. "All right. If you're sure I shouldn't stay."

His stomach still churned, and Brock didn't want to puke in front of Caspian. He swiped at his mouth, hoping he could hold back. "Yeah. You have nothing to do with this and I'm sure you have other things to do with your time. I'll see you tonight."

With another nod, Caspian accepted his keys. "Okay. Be careful." He kissed Brock's cheek.

Brock watched him go with his heart in his throat. One day soon, they would have to talk about them. It wouldn't happen with a headless body only feet away. It was best if Brock focused on the case in front of him. Tonight, though, he would have his moment with Caspian. It was time they made things real.

CASPIAN SPENT HIS AFTERNOON pacing the floor. He had gotten lucky with his last-second spell to behead that zombie. It looked to be a fairly recent turn, so—likely—in autopsy, he would just look like a crazy cannibal. Caspian couldn't keep taking risks. He had to live in this town. Caspian didn't want to end up back in New Orleans because he couldn't be himself anywhere else. He liked this weird little town filled with cheating spouses and hopeless romantics. Caspian stopped pacing. He liked Brock. It was time he stopped pretending he didn't. Caspian didn't know where to go with that. Margo would likely turn over in her grave.

A knock landed on the door, pulling Caspian from his musings. Caspian answered. Brock stood on the other side. His jacket was gone, and his sleeves were rolled up to his elbows. He looked tired. For a moment, they simply stared at each other.

"Hi."

A smile pulled at the corners of Caspian's mouth. "Hi."

Brock shuffled from foot to foot, looking adorably nervous. "So, are you ready to bob for apples and eat kettle corn?"

"Not really." But he would if that was what it took to spend more time with Brock.

"Thank god. One headless guy a day is enough for me," Brock said, stepping over the threshold and shocking Caspian.

Caspian's house was warded against intrusion. No one could come inside without invitation, which meant one thing. This house was meant to be Brock's house too. Caspian didn't have time to reel with that discovery. Brock kicked the door closed behind him and overcame Caspian. Their mouths met, and they immediately tore at each other's clothes. All the times Caspian had growled and scowled at Brock rose to the surface, revealing Caspian's irritation for what it was: unwanted lust. He wasn't supposed to feel this way about any authority figure. Caspian didn't want to fall for someone he would have to keep his magic hidden from for the rest of his life. That's why his kind almost always stuck with their own. He had too many potions and natural abilities he would have to keep secret. Caspian didn't want to want this.

His body and heart didn't care about any amount of logic. He was on fire.

"Where's your bedroom?" Brock asked between kisses.

Caspian took Brock's hand and led him toward the bedroom. Brock didn't make small talk. He simply towed Caspian into his arms and took him down onto the bed the moment they were close enough to do so. Brock's hands were everywhere. Despite his best efforts not to use his magic, Caspian used a little umph to help undress Brock a bit faster.

Brock kissed his way down Caspian's body. "Where do you keep your condoms?"

Caspian's mind froze. "Um. I don't have any."

Brock's head lifted. Their gazes met. "You don't?"

Caspian shook his head. Not only was he impervious to diseases, but Caspian also didn't sleep around. "No." He tried to explain. Even to his ears, he sounded uncomfortable. "Yeah, I don't… I mean, there's no one."

Brock nodded, as if he understood. He rolled away. Disappointment washed over Caspian. It was hard being different from everyone else. He liked not having competition here, but it was lonely being the only warlock for hundreds of miles.

Brock picked his jeans up off the floor. Defeat weighed heavily on Caspian's chest. Brock found his wallet and dug out a condom and a tiny sample-sized lube. A bright smile lit Brock's face. "Thank god. It's been so long; I couldn't remember if I had anything in my wallet."

Relief took Caspian's breath. Brock wasn't leaving. He crawled between Caspian's thighs and stared down at Caspian. "You're gorgeous. I could stare at you all day."

Caspian fought an unexpected blush. "Thank you. The feeling is mutual." He really could. Brock was one of those guys who was always perfectly put together. His hair was always styled, and his clothes always matched. He had a polish Caspian could never achieve. Caspian always wanted to touch him. He smelled nice too.

Brock slowly lowered his head.

Caspian watched him until the very last second. His eyes didn't close until their lips met. The muscles in his stomach clenched. His heart swelled with emotion. He didn't want this to be a one-night stand. Brock ran his hand down Caspian's torso, shaping every inch of Caspian, as if he had wanted to do so for a long time. A sharp pain took Caspian's breath when Brock nipped at his bottom lip. Then, in a flash, Caspian found himself on his stomach and clinging to the headboard while Brock kissed and bit a path down his body. He heard plastic crinkle as teeth sank into his ass cheek. Caspian's spine bowed. His skin burned.

Brock dragged Caspian's hips back and up until Caspian was on his knees. Wet fingers probed his asshole, stretching him. Moans vibrated in Caspian's throat. Then the blunt, wide head of Brock's cock pressed against the tight ring of muscles surrounding Caspian's asshole. Caspian fought the urge to beg. Brock thrust. A cry tore from Caspian's lips at the sudden intrusion.

"Fuck. I'm sorry. Damn. You feel good." Brock held still, giving Caspian time to adjust. "I'm sorry," he said again, but his hips rolled, belying his words.

Caspian clung to the headboard as Brock thrust again. He hit right where Caspian wanted him. A moan escaped him. Caspian squeezed his eyes closed and fought the magic inside him that wanted to rise to the surface. Cries that were out of his control reverberated from the walls as Brock slammed inside him over and over again. His dick leaked onto the mattress. Caspian's skin felt too tight. Pressure built, drawing his balls up as the spring inside him wound tighter. Caspian bit into his pillow. Electricity popped and crackled around his hands. He knew without looking there would a slight blue glow emanating from his palms. To give his powers an outlet, Caspian muttered an ancient spell beneath his breath, adding to the pleasure of their coupling.

Brock made a strangled sound.

Ecstasy tore through Caspian. Cum shot from his cock, soaking the blankets beneath him. Caspian openly humped the air, taking what he wanted from Brock's dick.

Brock's thrusts turned almost violent as he came. Indecipherable words came out in gasps from Brock's lips. His fingers dug into Caspian's skin with enough force to leave bruises. All Caspian knew was euphoria. Wave after wave of tiny deaths took him. He gasped his way through the multiple orgasms his spell created. Later, he would pat himself on the back for the earthquake-worthy orgasm he knew Brock experienced. Brock would never have another orgasm without thinking of him. Right now, Caspian couldn't think at all. The moment owned him. They collapsed into a heap of sweaty limbs. Brock placed light kisses on Caspian's ear—like he couldn't stop silently praising him.

"Wow. Goddamn. That was. You are. Goddamn. I'm shook."

A chuckle escaped Caspian. He couldn't stop it from happening. In all his years, he had never been happier than he was in that moment with a rambling Brock sweating all over him. He never wanted the night to end.

With darkness surrounding them, Brock held Caspian. He couldn't stop petting and kissing him. Never in all his thirty-six years had he experienced anything like sex with Caspian. His orgasm had been so intense, he swore he came several times and lost sight in one eye for a minute. In one encounter, Brock knew it was over for him. Well, honestly, before they had sex, Brock had already known he had met the one. But after sex, Caspian might have to physically toss him out if he wanted to rid himself of Brock. In his mind, Brock had already moved in, and they were six months into a forever marriage. This was the one for him. There was no going back.

“How did things go after I left?”

Brock stroked Caspian’s stomach and kissed the shell of his ear one more time because he couldn’t stop. “Uneventful. We didn’t find Frank, but we found his blood and other chunks of him around the mill. There’s little doubt he’s dead, as you said. It looks like he just had an unfortunate encounter with a crazy transient. I don’t think anyone else is in danger.”

Caspian nodded. He turned his head and kissed Brock, making Brock’s heart swell. "You were brave today. Thank you for keeping me safe."

Damn. Brock didn't think Caspian had needed him at all, but he loved hearing the praise. Caspian was intoxicating and addicting. Brock never wanted to be anywhere else. "I would never let anything happen to you." That much was absolutely true. Whether or not Caspian recognized it, he belonged to Brock. Brock would give his life to keep Caspian safe. "I have a question, though."

Caspian hummed against Brock's lips, trying to kiss him into silence.

This was too important for Brock to let Caspian distract him. He held Caspian's jaw, forcing Caspian to meet his stare. Caspian looked slightly nervous. Brock couldn't have that. They had danced around each other for too long now. "Would you be mine? Like officially? I mean, like I only date you and you only date me, and if people ask, I get to say you're my boyfriend."

A smile exploded across Caspian's face. "Yeah. I'd like that."

Happiness had Brock springing into action. He lunged, covering Caspian's body with his and capturing his mouth. Their tongues met and brushed. Their hard cocks strained to get closer like they hadn't already blown once tonight. Brock couldn't wait to get started on this forever thing. They were one thousand percent meant to be. He had never been happier.

CASPIAN'S HEAD WAS COMPLETELY in the clouds. He knew he should pay closer attention to his client, but it was hard, so hard with Brock nearby. His tiny shop seemed hotter and smaller than usual. Caspian fought the urge to scream for Clara to leave so he could properly fuck the man who owned one hundred percent of Caspian's thoughts.

"So I started seeing someone from work."

Caspian hummed. He already knew, since he'd drunk his potion already today, Clara still wasn't seeing the right person from work.

"I really think she's the one."

"She's not the one."

Clara's shoulders fell at Caspian's claim. "Really? Naomi is great. She's fun and energetic."

"Naomi Gray?" Brock asked from his spot by the door.

Clara turned in her seat. "Yeah. You know her too?"

Brock nodded. "She's sleeping with Susan and Geoff Tolbert behind each of their backs. It's actually been pretty crazy to watch for the past year."

"Seriously? Fuck. Why am I having such a tough time finding the right person?"

Probably because she had bad taste, but Caspian couldn't say that. "You need to open your mind to someone who might not be that exciting but who will treat you like a queen."

Clara nodded, looking thoughtful. "Okay. I'll think about it. Same time next week?"

Caspian smiled. "You're already on my calendar." They said their goodbyes while Caspian barely held on to his patience. Even after five months of dating, Caspian never got enough of spending time with Brock. Brock had moved in with Caspian six weeks ago, and even so, Caspian wanted to quit his job to live like a mole stuck to Brock's back. He had never been this addicted to anyone. Brock was a sickness.

Brock waited until they were alone to focus a knowing smile on Caspian. "Jesus. She's really going to date the entire town before she gets to poor Scott."

Caspian snorted. "It's job security for me, so whatever. Do you have another case for me?"

Brock nodded. "I have a case of missing you with a huge side of being completely and sickeningly in love with you."

"Same," Caspian admitted, even as a part of him hid in fear. As much as he couldn't live without Brock, there was still a part of him hiding and Caspian hated it. Margo had said he would know when he had met the one, because his soulmate would accept him. He wasn't so sure Brock would accept that Caspian could do way more than simply see into the future.

Brock overcame him and kissed him. Caspian clung to the suit that perfectly molded Brock's body. Brock's lips moved from Caspian's mouth to his ear. He licked. "You should do it just this one time."

"Do what?" Even to Caspian's ears, he sounded breathless.

"You should look into your future and prove to yourself that I'm your soulmate."

With his earlier potion still running through his veins, Brock's words conjured a vision with no permission from Caspian. He saw Brock and him together. They were laughing. Wedding rings adorned their fingers as they kissed.

“Stop conjuring plants. I’m the one who gets stuck watering them.”

“I can’t help it. My magic needs somewhere to go.”

A gasp tore from Caspian. They were soulmates. Not only were they destined to marry, but Brock would also accept his magic and keep his secrets.

Brock’s eyes danced with laughter. “I’m right, aren’t I?”

“Yes.”

Brock’s smile faltered at the open shock in Caspian’s voice. “Why do you sound like that? Aren’t you happy being with me?”

At the hurt in Brock's voice, Caspian scrambled to set aside his surprise. He could muse over his vision later. Right now, the love of his life needed his reassurance. "Of course I'm happy with you. That's not what caught me off guard. We were married. I never dreamed you'd get up off your ass and propose."

A laugh burst from Brock. "Why do I have to be the one to propose? You're perfectly capable of asking."

Caspian's cheeks hurt from smiling. He had never been happier in his life. "Fine. You should marry me."

Brock snorted. "That's not a proposal." He unbuttoned his jacket and reached inside the inner pocket. As Brock came out with a ring, he dropped to one knee. "This is a proposal. Caspian Moonchild, will you marry me?"

Even as Caspian nodded in shock, he wondered what in the hell had happened to his life. Five short months ago, he had vowed to steer clear of any law enforcement. Now, he just agreed to marry an agent. Not only that, but he also couldn't wait to tie himself to this amazing man.

Brock kissed him. Things turned heated faster than usual. Caspian already had plans to lock the door and celebrate with a little multiple orgasms spell he had come to rely on a tad too much. Brock's cellphone rang, interrupting them. With a growl, Brock pulled away and answered.

“Special Agent Brock Wray.” His gaze moved to Caspian. He held Caspian’s stare. “Yeah. I’m on my way.” He stuffed his phone back inside his pocket. “Are you interested in a man-sized dog who walks on two legs and is eating everyone’s cattle?”

Fuck. A werewolf. “Sure. I’ve got time.”

With a smile, Brock pulled Caspian to his feet. “It’s probably just a coyote or some other wild dog, but the strange and unusual is your specialty. Plus, it gives me an excuse to spend the day with you.”

Caspian was all in. He would always accept any case that allowed him to steal more time with Brock. Plus, someone had to keep his man safe. No one watched Brock's backside more thoroughly than Caspian. Caspian had seen their future, and it was beautiful. He would happily fight a werewolf for a shot at that life. There was nothing Caspian wouldn't do for Brock. There was nothing he wouldn't do for their love.

Please consider leaving a review at the retailer where you purchased this book. Reviews really help with a book's visibility, which allows me to continue writing more stories. Thank you, Charity.

About the Author

CHARITY PARKERSON IS AN award-winning and multi-published author with several companies. Born with no filter from her brain to her mouth, she decided to take this odd quirk and insert it in her characters.

*Eight-time Readers' Favorite Award Winner

*2015 Passionate Plume Award Finalist

*2013 Reviewers' Choice Award Winner

*2012 ARRA Finalist for Favorite Paranormal Romance

*Five-time winner of The Mistress of the Darkpath

Connect with her online:

*Sign up for her newsletter: https://sendfox.com/charityparkerson

*Join her readers' group on Facebook: http://bit.ly/CharitysTribe

*Website: https://www.charityparkerson.com

*A list of her social media accounts and giveaways all in one place: http://hy.page/charityparkerson

Made in the USA
Columbia, SC
14 April 2022